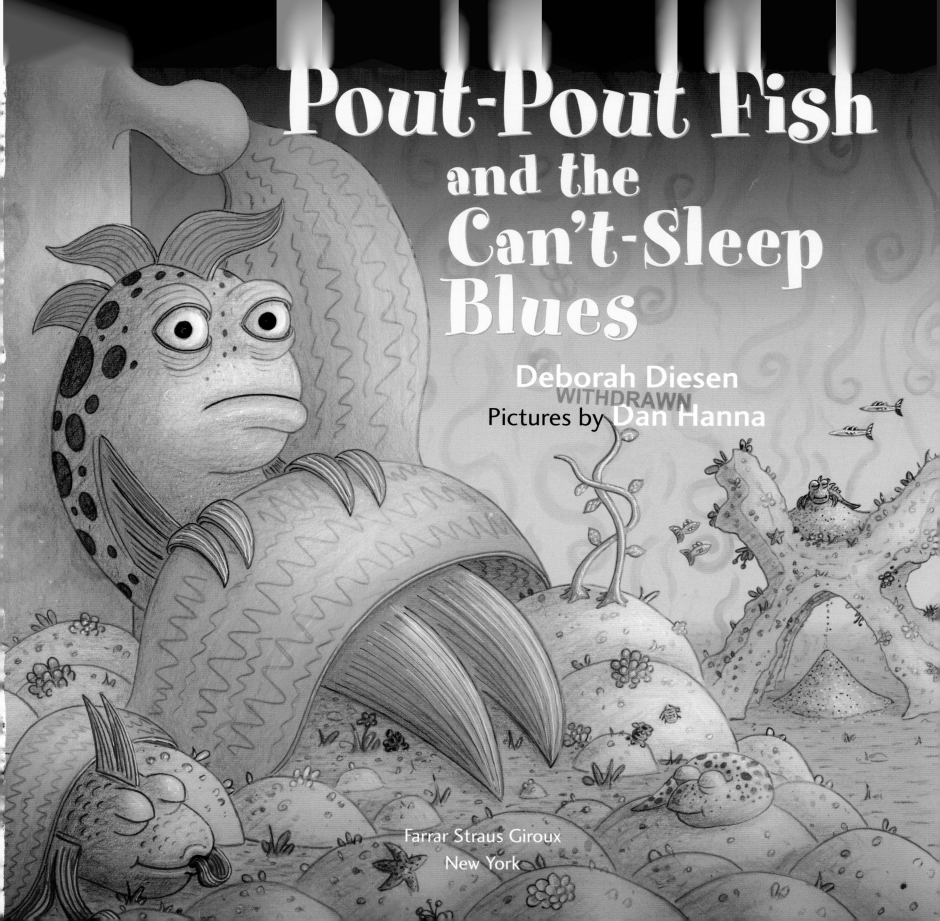

Pout-Pout Fish
and the
Can't-Sleep
Blues

Deborah Diesen

Pictures by Dan Hanna

Farrar Straus Giroux

New York

For Ginger, who taught me a thing or two about catnaps —D.D.

For Cause and dragonflies —D.H.

Farrar Straus Giroux Books for Young Readers
An imprint of Macmillan Publishing Group, LLC
175 Fifth Avenue, New York, NY 10010

Color separations by Embassy Graphics
Printed in China by RR Donnelley Asia Printing Solutions Ltd.,
Dongguan City, Guangdong Province
Designed by Roberta Pressel
First edition, 2018
10 9 8 7 6 5 4 3 2 1

mackids.com

Library of Congress Cataloging-in-Publication Data

Names: Diesen, Deborah, author. | Hanna, Dan, illustrator.
Title: The pout-pout fish and the can't-sleep blues / Deborah Diesen ;
    pictures by Dan Hanna.
Description: First edition. | New York : Farrar Straus Giroux, 2018. |
    Summary: Mr. Fish cannot fall asleep, but with help from his underwater
    friends, he finds a bedtime routine.
Identifiers: LCCN 2017013638 | ISBN 9780374304034 (hardcover)
Subjects: | CYAC: Stories in rhyme. | Fishes—Fiction. | Bedtime—Fiction. |
    Sleep—Fiction. | Marine animals—Fiction.
Classification: LCC PZ8.3.D565 Poj 2018 | DDC [E]—dc23
    LC record available at https://lccn.loc.gov/2017013638

Our books may be purchased in bulk for promotional, educational, or
business use. Please contact your local bookseller or the Macmillan
Corporate and Premium Sales Department at (800) 221-7945 ext. 5442
or by e-mail at MacmillanSpecialMarkets@macmillan.com.

Goldy Fish Condos

Polypville Apartments

Burrowland Bungalows

Late one quiet evening
In the inky ocean deep,
Mr. Fish blub-blubbed:
"Oh, I can't get to sleep!"

His mind was fizzy-busy
And his fins were full of vim.
Though he *wanted* to be dozing,
There were zero Z's for him!

"I *can't* drop into dreamland.
I *can't* slide into snooze.
I'm wide awake. It's hard to take
The **can't-sleep blues**."

A sleepy voice spoke softly.
"Need some tips?" inquired Ms. Clam.
"Just watch and see, and soon you'll be
As drowsy as I am.

"Smooth your seaweed bedding,
Then imagine fluffy sheep.
Count them one to twenty,
And then presto: Fall asleep!"

Mr. Fish took the advice,
But he couldn't catch a snooze.
"Ms. Clam, I need more help!"
Ms. Clam replied . . .

Then a sleepy voice spoke softly.
"Here's an even better fix.
You will love," said Mr. Crab,
"All my get-to-sleep-quick tricks.

"Just put on purple pj's,
And five or six orange socks.
Then soothe your busy thinking
On a pillow made of rocks."

Mr. Fish took the advice,
But he couldn't catch a snooze.
"Mr. Crab, what *now*?"
Mr. Crab replied . . .

Then a sleepy voice spoke softly.
"Here is what I would suggest,
Guaranteed," said Mr. Eel,
"To yield a pleasant night's rest.

"First ripple to the left,
Then ripple to the right.
Next, swirl in a circle.
Swoosh, swoosh! Nighty-night!"

Mr. Fish took the advice,
But he couldn't catch a snooze.
"Mr. Eel, what's the deal?"
Mr. Eel replied . . .

Then a sleepy voice spoke softly.
"For your slumber in the sea,
Here's a plan," said Mrs. Squid,
"That always does the trick for me.

"Just widen out your eyes
And give four quick, tiny blinks.
Then slowly close your lids:
Automatic forty winks!"

Mr. Fish took the advice,
But he couldn't catch a snooze.
"Mrs. Squid, more ideas?"
Mrs. Squid replied . . .

Then Mr. Fish heard nothing,
Just a symphony of snore.
He *still* couldn't sleep.
He felt *worse* than before!

"I took *all* of their suggestions,
Which I followed to a T.
Their methods worked for them,
But they did not work for me.

"I don't know what to do!"
He sank down in the kelp.
"What good is good advice?
It does *not* always help!"

Then a sparkly voice emerged.
"Mr. Fish, you're partly right."
The voice was dear Miss Shimmer's.
Her smile was kind and bright.

"But take what you've been given,
And learn from what you've tried.
Then build your own solution:
Trust *yourself* as a guide.

"The best advice of all,"
Said Miss Shimmer to her friend,
"Is to learn what works for you
And make your *own* special blend!"

With that, she said good night
And departed from the scene.
Now Mr. Fish was ready
To create his own routine.

"I'll settle in my spot.
I'll smooth my seaweed bed.

"I'll smooch my Snoozy Snuggly,
Then I'll clear my busy head.

"I'll swoosh in gentle motion
In the ocean wide and deep.

"I'll close my eyes, fins tucked in,
And drift right off to sleep."

Mr. Fish had tried his best
To resolve his can't-sleep blues.

"Mr. Fish, how'd it go?"
Mr. Fish replied . . .